D0638839

SAPPHIRE the GREAT and the MEANING of Life

SAPPHIRE the GREAT and the MEANING of Life

Find your purpose!

Beverley Brenna

Illustrated by Tara Anderson

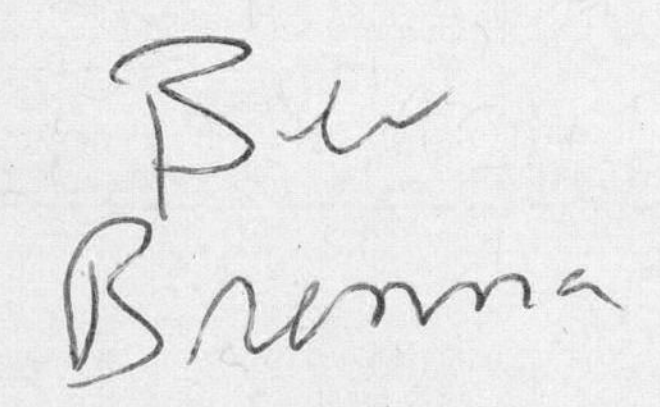

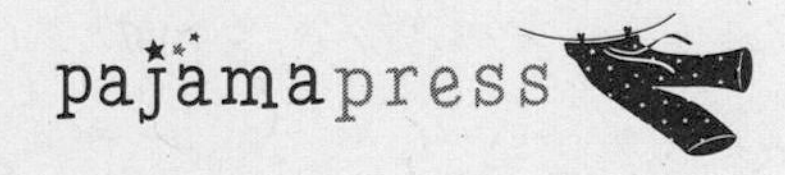

First published in Canada and the United States in 2019

This is a first edition.

10 9 8 7 6 5 4 3 2 1

www.pajamapress.ca info@pajamapress.ca

ONTARIO ARTS COUNCIL
CONSEIL DES ARTS DE L'ONTARIO
an Ontario government agency
un organisme du gouvernement de l'Ontario

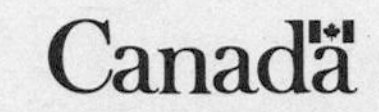

The publisher gratefully acknowledges the support of the Canada Council for the Arts and the Ontario Arts Council for its publishing program. We acknowledge the financial support of the Government of Canada through the Canada Book Fund (CBF) for our publishing activities.

Library and Archives Canada Cataloguing in Publication

Brenna, Beverley A., author

Sapphire the Great and the meaning of life / Beverley Brenna;
cover and interior illustrations, Tara Anderson.
ISBN 978-1-77278-069-7 (hardcover)

I. Anderson, Tara, illustrator II. Title.

PS8553.R382S38 2019 jC813'.54 C2018-905441-7

Publisher Cataloging-in-Publication Data (U.S.)

Names: Brenna, Beverley, 1962-, author.
Title: Sapphire the Great and the Meaning of Life / Beverley Brenna.
Description: Toronto, Ontario Canada : Pajama Press, 2019. | Summary: "Nine-year-old Jeannie buys a pet hamster (who shares narrating duties) after her parents separate when her father reveals that he is gay. Jeannie and her mother befriend a transgender neighbor, and the hamster becomes a calming influence on the characters, despite its own difficult quest to find the meaning of life" -- Provided by publisher.
Identifiers: ISBN 978-1-77278-069-7 (hardcover)
Subjects: LCSH: Divorced parents – Juvenile fiction. | Sexual minorities – Juvenile fiction. | Gay parents – Juvenile fiction. | Transgender people – Juvenile fiction. | BISAC: JUVENILE FICTION / Family / Marriage & Divorce. | JUVENILE FICTION / LGBT.
Classification: LCC PZ7.B746Sa |DDC 813.6 – dc23

Cover and interior illustrations—Tara Anderson
Cover design—Rebecca Bender
Text design—Lorena Gonzalez Guillen

Manufactured by Webcom
Printed in Canada

Pajama Press Inc.
181 Carlaw Ave. Suite 251 Toronto, Ontario Canada, M4M 2S1
Distributed in Canada by UTP Distribution
5201 Dufferin Street Toronto, Ontario Canada, M3H 5T8

Distributed in the U.S. by Ingram Publisher Services
1 Ingram Blvd. La Vergne, TN 37086, USA

For the real SAPPHIRE, wherever you may be

–B.B.

For Alice

–T.A

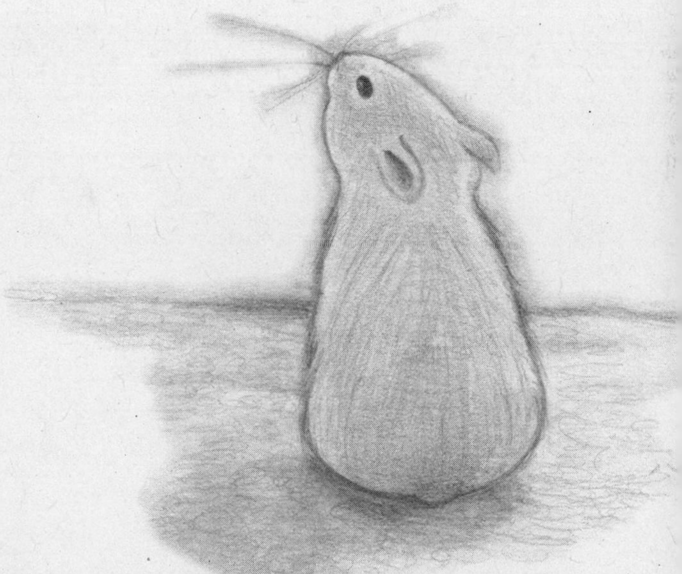

CHAPTER ONE

JEANNIE

The only good thing about today is that we're *finally* going to the Pet Store. Mom promised we'd go last week but then I forgot to do my chores, so the Pet Store got canceled. But it's back! Today it's back on the list!

First we have to get Alistair some new underwear. And I have to go along, because Mom says I can't stay in the car alone.

"I'm nine!" I yell at her as she parks the car. "I'm nine years old, FOR GOODNESS' SAKE."

"I'm aware of that," she says, opening the door and hauling me out.

"What could happen to me if I just stay in the car?" I argue.

"It's winter, Jeannie," she says. "It's cold, remember?"

"Oh, yeah," I say. She's right. I forgot about that.

Alistair's my brother and he should be able to buy underwear by himself because he's twelve and over five feet tall. But he hates going places. It's up to us, Mom says, to get him out of the house.

"How come Alistair's not getting out of the car?" I yell, kicking up snow with my ugly brown boots.

Mom opens Alistair's door and hauls him out too. I can tell she's getting angry. Her face is all red. Then I remember the Pet Store again.

"Alistair!" I yell. "C'mon! First underwear, then the Pet Store, remember?"

He stares at me, and his eyes look a little glassy.

"THE PET STORE," I yell, even louder. "Today I'm getting my hamster, Alistair! My CHRISTMAS HAMSTER."

His eye twitches and I know he's still thinking about that video game he was playing before we left. He was getting a lot of points and then it was time to go. I think my brother has an ADDICTION, but he doesn't want to admit it.

"Okay, let's get this done," Mom says, holding open the door to the mall. I duck under her arm, but Alistair grabs the door and makes her go first. Ever since Dad left, Alistair's been doing dumb things like that. As if he could ever take Dad's place.

Not Alistair.

Not anyone.

And now I feel awful. My stomach hurts and I start dragging my feet.

"Come on, Jeannie!" Mom says. "We only have a few minutes on the parking meter."

"I'm hungry," I say. It's what I always say when I start missing Dad.

"Well, there's a popcorn store in here somewhere," Mom replies. "After we get Alistair's things, we can stop there."

"You mean after we get ALISTAIR'S UNDERWEAR?" I yell.

"Shut up," Alistair says. "You don't have to be so loud."

"I'M NOT BEING LOUD," I yell. "**THIS IS LOUD.**"

"Mom!" yells Alistair.

She turns around and looks at us both. I suddenly think of her erasing Pet Store from the list.

"Okay, okay," I mumble. "Sorry. Sorry, Alistair. Sorry, Mom. Sorry, sorry, sorry."

"Fine," Mom says. "Just try to get along, you two."

"Sorry, Nose," I say.

Alistair laughs.

"Sorry, Ear," he answers. When we were little we used to call each other Nose and Ear all the time. I don't know who started it.

"Alistair's new underwear," I chant under my breath. It sort of rhymes, and I add a little tune to it as we walk along. "*Alistair's new underwear. Underwear's new Alistair,*" I sing.

We stop at the men's department and I look around, surprised.

"What are we doing in here?" I ask.

"Shhh," Mom says. "Your brother's growing up."

"He's not," I say.

"Shut up!" my brother says. His face is all red.

"Okay, okay," I say. "Just finish shopping and let's go to the Pet Store. Right? We're still going to the Pet Store. RIGHT, MOM?"

She looks at me, but she doesn't say anything. I cross my fingers. It's three weeks past Christmas, and she's promised me that hamster. I have to get it today. I just have to get it today!

"Mom!" I yell. "YOU PROMISED."

She turns her back on me and starts poking through packages of underwear. It's men's long underwear. I remember Dad had this stuff. He always put it on before he went to play hockey.

Dad.

Now I feel really awful. We might not even go to the Pet Store today! I pull on one of the clothes racks. Suddenly it leans backward, and the whole thing comes crashing down on top of me. Men's pajamas. I'm lying under a whole pile of men's pajamas.

"Jeannie!" Mom yells. I can see her erasing Pet Store. I can see her erasing Pet Store from the list right now.

CHAPTER TWO

SAPPHIRE

Here I am, sitting in my cage, waiting for something. The trouble is, I do not know what I am waiting for.

Today began like any other. I traversed the floor of the cage, rating the aspen shavings. I thought, just like I always do: *Fresh! Very Fresh! Not Fresh! Somewhat Fresh! Fresh! Fresh! Fresh! Not Fresh!* Then I dragged my food bowl to *Very Fresh!* And I buried the bowl and all its meager contents.

In my food bowl there are two Cheerios, three Rice Krispies, a fragment of apple, and one peanut. The peanuts are being offered more and more infrequently. Two weeks ago I was getting a couple of peanuts every day. Last week

I got three in total. This week I have had only one. I believe they are trying to send me a message.

After burying my food bowl I traversed the cage again, attempting to create a food puzzle. I do not want to solve the food puzzle too quickly so I dig into the bedding, uncover the food bowl, and eat the peanut. I then bury the food bowl a second time, unfortunately in the same place as before because of the limited amount of *Very Fresh*. Then I try to forget its location so that discovery is possible.

But I cannot forget. I know exactly where I put the food bowl. And it is calling me right now.

I sniff the air. I can still smell the peanut even though it is gone. I dig up the food bowl and look at it carefully, just in case there might be another peanut. There is not another peanut. But I knew there was not, so I am not disappointed.

Then I eat the fragment of apple, the three Rice Krispies, and the two Cheerios. Now the bowl is empty. And I am still waiting. But I do not know what I am waiting for.

I hope something happens soon.

But I am afraid it will not.

CHAPTER THREE

JEANNIE

Mom promised and promised that we'd go to the Pet Store today, and now we are not. We are not going to the Pet Store, even though it's been three weeks and I haven't spent my Christmas money. Dad said I could buy a hamster with it, or anything I wanted.

"I haven't spent ANY of it," I say for the millionth time.

Finally Alistair yells from the back seat, "Enough already!"

But I can't stop.

"YOU PROMISED! YOU PROMISED! YOU PROMISED!" I yell at Mom.

"Enough!" Alistair says again. "I'm getting a headache.

Let's just go there, Mom. Let's just go to the Pet Store and be done with it."

"She has to learn to behave," snaps Mom. "Clothes racks are not monkey bars. And crawling under the door of that change room was NOT okay."

"She thought I was in there," says Alistair. "I said the lock was stuck, and she thought she was helping. She didn't know that someone else was in the first one."

"That poor man," mutters Mom. "He nearly had a heart attack."

"*I* nearly had a heart attack!" I yell. "I thought Alistair was in there. And then I saw that man with his shirt off. He looked like a gorilla!"

There is a moment of silence. Then Alistair laughs. Then Mom laughs. Then I laugh, and suddenly we're going to the Pet Store! We're going there *right now*!

CHAPTER FOUR

SAPPHIRE

I feel as though I have been waiting for something all day but it is only noon. I know that it is noon because the light coming down onto my cage is from the big windows and that kind of light only lasts a short while. Then it will be afternoon and the sunlight will be gone. And then it will be night and even the ceiling light will be gone and it will be dark.

I do not like the dark. I am supposed to like it. I am supposed to like the dark because I am a hamster and all hamsters like the dark. But I do not. I do not like it at all.

I climb on top of the paper tube that someone has stuck in here and then I raise myself onto my back legs. I am as close to the noon sunlight as I can get. Warmth hums along the top of my head and I feel good. Sunlight. Pure sunlight is like a song. It sings against my fur. I start humming.

"What's wrong with that hamster?" someone asks. "The white one."

It is a man. It is a man's voice.

"I think he's sick," the man goes on. "His eyes are shut and he's kind of whimpering."

I stop singing and open my eyes. The man is bending down and looking at me through the bars of my cage. A little boy is there too, staring in.

Sick? I am not sick. I jump down from the paper tube and run around the cage as fast as I can. *Look! See me run! See how healthy I am!* When I stop running and look out of the cage, they are gone.

"We don't want a sick one," I hear the man say from a distance. "How about this little brown one over here? He's a cute one."

It is not fair that nobody wants me. I have been here the longest. I should be chosen first!

Is being chosen the only way to *Be Free?*

What if I never get chosen?

I lean against the bars of my cage and close my eyes. Then I bury my food bowl. It is the only thing I can think of to do. But burying it does not bring me much comfort. I know where it is. I can easily find it again. And it will still be empty.

"What is my purpose?" I whisper. "What is the meaning of life?" But nobody answers.

I lean against the bars of my cage but this time I keep my eyes open. On my side of the bars I am *Not Free*. On the other side of the bars I would *Be Free*.

"I wish I were *Free*," I whisper.

CHAPTER FIVE

JEANNIE

As soon as I see the puppies, I really want one.

"Mom!" I say. "LOOK AT THESE PUPPIES."

But she doesn't answer.

"MOM," I repeat.

"Jeannie. We're not here to get a dog," Mom says.

Then I see the kittens. But Alistair has already started sneezing.

Everyone in my family has allergies except me. Well, me and Dad, but I don't really know if Dad's still part of our family.

"Can we also get a snack somewhere?" I say. "After we get the hamster?" But Mom says nothing.

Dad hasn't been back since our family meeting two weeks ago. The family meeting when they told us they were getting separated. Not divorced. They didn't say divorced. They said separated.

"Like eggs?" I asked when they said it. I know how to separate eggs. And I know that you can put the two parts back together, like in an omelet or something.

"No," Mom said. "Not like eggs."

Dad hasn't been back since they told us. In two weeks he hasn't been back. Not even once.

"What about fish?" Mom is asking. "These fish are quite astonishing. Look at their huge eyeballs. I bet they can see super well. If I had eyes like that, I'd probably get my paperwork done in half the time."

"No!" I say. "I'm not having fish!"

"Look at the guppies. They're rainbow guppies! Look at their incredible tails!" Mom continues. "Wouldn't you like a guppy?"

"NO!" I cry. "I'm not having a stupid guppy! I'm getting a hamster, remember? The Christmas money was for a HAMSTER! And hamster food! And hamster shavings! AND A CAGE."

I pull the list out of my pocket so I'll remember all the things I need.

"Jeannie, you don't have to yell," Mom says. "I can hear you fine when you use your regular voice."

"Maybe you can hear me," I mutter. "But you're not really listening." I want to kick something with my stupid big boots, but I don't.

I walk away from the fish and along the side wall, where I see bags of wood shavings and lots of small cages. This is where the hamsters are.

I look in the first cage, but it's empty. I look in the second cage. It's empty too. I look in the third cage. At first I think it's empty, but then I see a little white ball of fluff over in the corner. As I look at it, the eyes pop open. At first I think they're black, but then I realize they're blue. Navy blue.

"Hello," I say. "Are you really a hamster? I've never seen a white hamster before!"

The hamster blinks. I think he sees me. I'm sure he sees me. Then I hear a kind of humming sound.

"Are you singing?" I say. "I like to sing too!"

The humming stops, and then it starts again.

"You are perfect!" I say. "I'm going to name you..." I try and think of a good name. *Hammy?* Too common. *Fluffy?* Also too common. *Harvey?* Harvey is my dad's name.

"Hey, did you see the snakes?" Alistair calls. "Jeannie, there's baby snakes over here!"

"I found the hamster I want," I call back. "I've found my hamster! MOM!"

"Well...," Mom says, looking over my shoulder at the hamster. "Well, he is a cute little guy. My goodness, look at his eyes! What will you name him?"

"Harvey Owens," I blurt.

"You...you're naming him after your father?" Mom says in a funny kind of voice.

"I can name my hamster whatever I want," I tell her. "You even said so."

"Well...," says Mom. "Well, we'd better get him paid for."

"But first we have to get all the stuff he needs!" I say, waving my list around. Then I read it out loud.

Food Dish
Hanging Water Bottle
Hamster Food
Cage
Wood Shavings
Wooden Toys (not plastic!)
And of course: Exercise Wheel!

We pick up all the supplies, and then I follow Mom to the cash register and take out my wallet. It's fat with all the money I've saved from Christmas, and from before Christmas, too, when I did extra chores.

The Pet-Store lady gets a cardboard box and comes back to help me get Harvey Owens ready for the trip. But when we reach his cage, I see that the top of the cage is open.

The top of the cage is open and my hamster is gone!

"HARVEY OWENS!" I yell.

CHAPTER SIX

SAPPHIRE

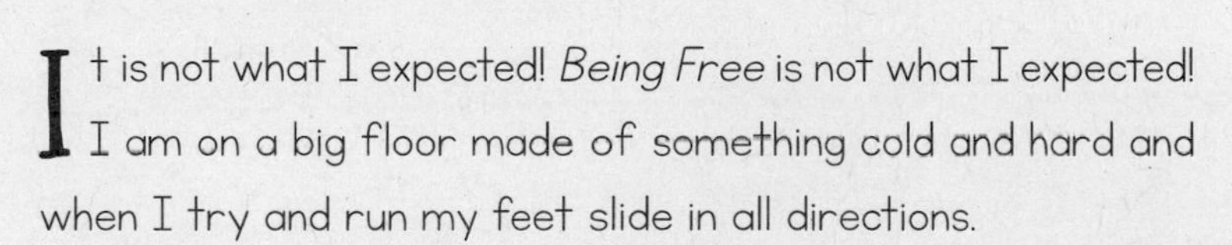

It is not what I expected! *Being Free* is not what I expected! I am on a big floor made of something cold and hard and when I try and run my feet slide in all directions.

I try harder to run. I slip. I slide. Suddenly I do a triple flip and then I coast into the wall and hit my head. And I cannot get up. There are lots of bad smells and bad noises. I hear hissing. And barking. The fur on the back of my neck prickles. I am afraid. I squeeze my eyes shut. And then I open them again.

But my eyes do not work properly! Everything around me is a big white blur. I still feel as if I am in some sort of cage. I stumble to my feet. I try even harder to run. My legs burn.

And then I see a hand. The hand is reaching toward me. I do the only thing I can think of to do.

I bite.

CHAPTER SEVEN

JEANNIE

"Ow!" I yell. "DON'T BITE."

I look at my pinky finger. There is no blood, but it hurts.

I look at Harvey Owens.

"What did you do that for?" I say.

His navy blue eyes stare directly at me. And I know. I know right away. He didn't mean to bite me. He didn't mean it.

I carefully scoop him up.

"That was an accident, right?" I ask.

He blinks. And then he starts to purr. His whole body kind of vibrates in my hand.

"Hey, Alistair," I call to my brother. "Meet Harvey-the-Hamster Owens!"

Alistair comes over and looks at my hamster.

"Cute," he says. "But it's dumb to name him that." Then he calls, "Hey, Mom! Can I have a baby snake? Dad had a snake when he was a kid."

"No," she says. "Let's go home."

The car is cold. Harvey Owens is in a little box on my lap and I keep the lid shut. But I tell him that soon it'll be okay. Soon we'll be home and he'll be in his new cage with lots of water and food and wood shavings.

I think I hear him scurrying around in the box, but the car heater is loud and I can't be sure.

CHAPTER EIGHT

SAPPHIRE

I hate the cold. I hate the dark. And I hate the car. It rumbles. It shakes. I slide from side to side in the box. Even though I am out of my cage, I am still *Not Free*.

"My name is Jeannie," the girl says through the slit in the top of the box. "And your name is Harvey Owens."

That is a dumb name to call me, I say. But I don't think she hears.

My mother did not have time to name me. There were nine of us in the nest. There was a lot of scratching. I lived in that nest for twenty-one days. Then someone brought me to the pet store. I do not miss my family. And I am sure they do not miss me.

Now the car is starting to warm up. We are still moving but the girl opens the box and pets my back. I love being petted. I hear her singing.

"*I love you,*" she is singing. "*And you love me.*"

I start to sing along.

I love apples, I sing. *And I love Cheerios.*

Suddenly there is a loud bang and everything is spinning and I am sliding around inside the box and it is terrifying and when we come to a stop I bump hard against Jeannie's hand.

And I do the only thing I can think of to do.

I bite.

CHAPTER NINE

JEANNIE

"WHAT THE HECK!" Mom is yelling.

The front of our car is wrecked. And the big white truck that hit us is backing away.

"Jeannie, are you okay?" Mom asks me. "Alistair, are you okay?"

We nod.

Mom leaps out of the car.

"Stop!" she yells. Then she runs over to the truck. It stops moving. An old woman gets out. The old woman looks over at us, and then she looks at Mom. She's very tall. A lot taller than Mom; I think she's even taller than Dad.

Mom and the woman talk for a minute, and then Mom starts writing things down on some paper she's taken from her purse. The old woman comes over and inspects the front of our car. Then she looks through the window at me and Alistair. And then she taps at my window.

"Don't open it," Alistair says. "She could be crazy."

The woman taps at the window again.

I press the button and open the window.

"I am so sorry," she rumbles. "I didn't see the stop sign. It's all my fault."

"That's okay," I say.

"Don't talk to her," Alistair whispers from the back seat. "Don't say anything that could be used in court!"

"I have to close the window," I tell her. "So my hamster doesn't get cold."

"You're bleeding!" booms the woman. Her voice sounds like thunder. I look down at my hand. Blood is dripping from my finger. I look into the box and Harvey Owens is in there looking up at me with those blue, blue eyes.

"Ow," I say to Harvey Owens. "My finger hurts!"

The woman takes a Band-Aid out of her purse and waves it through the open window.

"I feel terrible!" she says.

"It's not your fault," I tell her, taking the Band-Aid and putting it on my finger.

"Don't say that!" warns Alistair.

"I'm going to talk with your mom now," says the woman. "And see what I can do to help."

I close my window. Then Mom hurries back to the car, opens her door, and turns the engine off. That's when I know we're going to be here a while.

"That hamster smells," says Alistair.

"Shut up," I tell him.

My feet get cold first, and then the rest of me. I don't know what we're waiting for, but then Mom tells us we need a tow truck. The tow truck takes so long that finally the woman offers to drive us home.

"Bad idea," warns Alistair. "Strangers!"

"We met once at work. And we're sort of neighbors," Mom says. "So therefore...we can't just sit here and freeze."

I look into the box. Harvey Owens is shivering.

"Let's go," I say. "DON'T FORGET YOUR UNDERWEAR, ALISTAIR."

"Shut up," he says, but he pulls out his bag as well as the hamster cage and supplies. Then we pile into the back seat of the truck while Mom gets into the front. I very carefully hold the box that contains Harvey Owens.

"She could definitely be a kidnapper," Alistair is muttering.

"This is Anna Conda," says Mom.

Alistair snorts and Mom turns around and gives us the hairy eyeball.

The woman turns around as well. She has pale whiskers sticking out of her chin.

"We'll get you home safe and sound," the woman says. "Ford and I."

"Ford?" I ask.

"My truck. I've named him Ford because…well…he is a Ford," she says. "I'm so sorry about all of this. It's the least I can do to make up for all the trouble."

"Perfume," grumbles Alistair as he buries his nose in his arm.

"Could you turn up the heat?" I ask. "Harvey Owens is still cold."

"Absolutely," says the woman. "Harvey is a—a hamster, right?"

"Right," I tell her.

"You won't let Harvey out of the box, now will you?" the woman says. "I am remembering that hamsters are quite a bit like mice. And so you won't open the lid of the box—" She gives a little shiver.

"I won't," I promise. "Harvey Owens is going to stay in this box until we get home!"

"I don't know what possessed her to name it that," Mom mutters.

The woman laughs. It's a big laugh.

"It is very nice alliteration," she says. "Harvey Hamster."

"Harvey the Hamster Owens, ma'am," I tell her. "Harvey Owens, for short."

"I like it!" she replies. "Please, call me Anna."

"Anna…Conda?" says Alistair. "Like…*anaconda*? The snake?"

"Absolutely!" bellows the woman. She gives that big laugh again and waves one hand around. There's a gold watch on her wrist and it gleams. "Snakes are my favorite animal next to trucks," she says.

"Your parents must have had a sense of humor," says Alistair.

"Alistair!" cries Mom.

"No worries," Anna says. "I paid for the name change. My parents called me something else, but it didn't work for me."

We pull up in front of our house and Anna waves her hand around at all of us. The gold watch gleams even brighter.

"Farewell for now," she says.

"I like your watch," I say.

"It was a prize," she says. "For figure skating. Just a little prize, but very, very precious to me."

"I like skating too!" I tell her.

"Now, please let me know if I can do anything else to help," Anna says to Mom. And then she looks back at me.

"Keep that little box shut tightly now, on your way out, yes? I wouldn't want anything like a mouse loose in here!"

"Thanks for the ride," Mom says, opening the door of the truck. "We'll let you know what the adjustor says."

"I'll be happy to pay whatever costs you have," Anna calls. "For anything. Just let me know."

We get out of the truck and go inside. I put my hamster box on the kitchen table and lift the lid just to make sure he's okay. Then I pour wood shavings into the cage and put in his food dish. Then I carefully fill his water bottle and hang it on the side of the cage. When I take out my wallet, it's a lot lighter than before. That stuff wasn't cheap, and I'll have to keep on buying food and wood shavings. Maybe I'll need a job!

"She looked rich," I say to Mom. "Maybe—"

"Don't even think about it," Mom says in a tired voice.

"Well, she offered," I say. "She offered to pay for stuff."

"She looked like a man," Alistair says.

CHAPTER TEN

SAPPHIRE

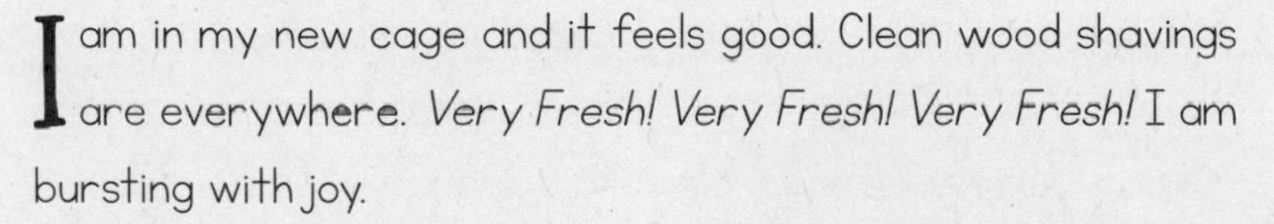

I am in my new cage and it feels good. Clean wood shavings are everywhere. *Very Fresh! Very Fresh! Very Fresh!* I am bursting with joy.

Jeannie has given me clean water and filled my food bowl. I count three Cheerios, two pieces of apple, and a big piece of carrot. And it is not even suppertime!

Then Jeannie disappears but her brother Alistair is looking in at me. He opens the top of my cage and pokes me in the back. He does not poke me hard but it surprises me. I take a step forward. He pokes me again.

I do the only thing I can think of to do.

I bite.

"Ow!" Alistair yells and pulls his hand away. Now he is gone. And Jeannie is gone. And my cage door is open. *An Exit!* I carefully climb on top of the carrot and stand on my back feet and reach up with my claws. And suddenly, I am out of the cage. I am *Free* for the second time today!

Now is the time! Now is the time for me to do something really great!

I dart across the table, jump down onto a chair, and then close my eyes and dive. Luckily I land on something soft. It is a slipper. I scamper off the slipper and then I stop and sniff the air. I smell a lot of things. Apples. Cheerios. Peanuts. *Very Fresh. Very Fresh. Very Fresh!*

The stronger the smell of food, the hungrier I am. At this moment my appetite has made me delirious. I eat a few crumbs and then I run over to the cupboards to see if they can be climbed. They cannot. I run along the front of the cupboards looking for an *Entry*. Nothing.

At some point in my search I am startled by a screech and then I hear breaking glass. I dart around a puddle on the floor and run under the refrigerator.

"Jeannie!" her mother is yelling. "That hamster got out!"

And now I am here, under the refrigerator. It is warm and dark. The motor hums and the appliance looms above me. All at once I feel very small and weak. The excitement I had because of an *Exit* vanishes. I am inclined to sleep.

Sleep has always been my first response to trauma. My eyes shut. I doze.

Suddenly I hear something scraping along the floor and I wake up just in time to vault over the wooden ruler as it sweeps from one side of the fridge to the other. Someone is trying to force me out.

I scurry to the back wall and make myself as small as possible. After a few minutes, when the ruler has not returned, I notice piles of crumbs and pieces of old lettuce back here. There is even a chocolate chip. I gnaw on it. As the caffeine from the chocolate courses through my veins, I begin to worry. What about water? What if the fridge collapses and I am crushed by its weight?

I nose around the food scraps. *Not Fresh. Not Fresh. Not Fresh.* Suddenly I realize what I have done. I am still *Not Free*—I have simply acquired a bigger cage.

I see the ruler sweeping back. I scamper ahead of it and then I make my decision.

So here I am, back in the hamster cage. I have been allowed to keep a carrot top that I found on the floor and I begin to chew. There is nothing so calming as a wilted bit of carrot. But am I happy?

I hum all the questions I have been thinking for as long as I can remember: *What is the meaning of life? Why am I here? Who am I (essentially)? What is my greater purpose?*

I feel dizzy with all I do not know. After a while Jeannie picks up my cage and carries it into her room, where she puts it on her dresser. When the lights go out, I become increasingly agitated and dart around my cage. I do not like the dark but I am supposed to be nocturnal so I give it my best shot. I climb into the exercise wheel and run. The wheel goes around and around but I stay in the same spot. How fun is this? Soon I am bored and tired. I jump off the wheel and lie down in a nest of wood shavings that I scraped together with my back feet.

I thought perhaps the cage would have become bigger in my brief absence. It has not. It has become smaller.

CHAPTER ELEVEN

JEANNIE

Mom says I can't take Harvey Owens to show-and-tell tomorrow. She says we have to watch him carefully so that he does not get out of his cage again. She also says that Dad isn't coming by to see him. Or any of us. At least, he's not coming by tonight.

"WHY CAN'T DAD COME OVER TONIGHT?" I ask for the tenth time.

"Jeannie," says Mom. "We've already talked about this."

"BUT WHY?" I say. "He doesn't even know about my hamster!"

"Well," sighs Mom. "Maybe we could phone him."

I don't know why she always sounds so tired. We've barely done anything today.

"Can we phone him right now?" I ask.

She gets out her phone and taps in a number.

"Here you go," she says.

I imagine Dad's ring. It's ducks quacking. After a few seconds, he answers.

"Hi?" says Dad.

"Dad!" I shout. "GUESS WHAT?"

"Hi, Jeannie!" he says.

"I got a new hamster!"

"Great!" he says. "Your Christmas hamster."

"Yes!" I say. And then there is a silence. My stomach growls.

"When are you coming to see him?" I ask.

"Well, your mom and I have a few things to work out...," he says.

"About getting put back together?" I say, thinking about omelets.

"No. No, about how we're going to...well...just things," he says. Then he says something that I can't quite hear. And it sounds as if someone else is there with him, because I can hear another man's voice.

"Who is that?" I ask. "Who's there?"

I can also hear birds. I hear birds singing.

"Where are you?" I ask. "When are you coming home? When can we go skating again?"

"I'd better let you get back to...to... I'd better let you go for now, honey," he says. "But I'll see you and your hamster soon, okay? And tell Alistair I love him."

"And you love me," I say.

"Of course. I love you all," he says.

"But just not Mom."

"What?" he says.

"Just not Mom. You don't love Mom," I say, and my voice sounds sharp as a skate blade.

"It's complicated, honey," says Dad. "Bye, then. Bye for now."

I slam the phone onto the counter.

"He's not coming over," I say. Then I burst into tears and run into my bedroom.

Harvey Owens comes over to the side of his cage and looks at me. He's probably sad for me. He probably wants me to stop crying, so I do.

"Don't feel bad," I whisper. "Dad will come soon. He misses us. He'll come back soon."

Harvey Owens blinks at me and I take him out of the cage. His fur is so soft and so warm. I bury my nose in it. He smells fresh, like a forest.

I hold him gently with both hands, and Harvey Owens starts purring.

"Jeannie," my mom says. She's standing in the hallway looking in at us. "Are you okay?"

I don't answer at first. Then I say, "We're sad that Dad isn't coming over. But maybe he'll come over tomorrow."

"Well, not just yet," says Mom. "We're trying to decide how to…but maybe. Maybe he will."

She comes in and sits beside me on the bed.

"This little guy is really quite pretty," she says. "Look at those eyes." Then she reaches out and tickles him under the chin.

"It'll be okay," she says. "You'll see."

I feel like crying again. But I don't. I look at Harvey Owens instead.

"I can't find the wooden hamster toys I bought him," I say, sniffing just a little. "I forgot to put them in his cage, and now I can't find them. And I'm going to need a bigger allowance so I can afford all the food and wood shavings I'll need to buy later. And I hate those old brown boots—"

"Oh, Jeannie," Mom sighs. "Why does everything have to be so difficult?"

CHAPTER TWELVE

SAPPHIRE

Jeannie's mother is scratching me under the chin. And I do not like it.

It tickles.

So I do the only thing I can think of to do.

I bite.

CHAPTER THIRTEEN

JEANNIE

Mom has a big fit. But just because he bites doesn't mean Harvey Owens is a bad hamster. I mean, hamsters are supposed to bite.

"But they're not supposed to bite people!" Mom snaps as she stalks out of the room to get a Band-Aid.

"Yeah!" Alistair calls from his bedroom. I hear the music start on his video game. The game he's been ADDICTED to ever since Dad left.

"Maybe that hamster has rabies!" Alistair hollers.

"Shut up!" I yell. "SHUT UP."

If Harvey Owens keeps biting people, Mom says he'll have to go back to the Pet Store.

"That isn't going to happen!" I mutter. "THAT ISN'T GOING TO HAPPEN."

I slam my bedroom door. Then I open the door and slam it harder. My lamp falls over and I kick it into the closet. Who needs lamps!

Then I take out a sheet of paper. I make a chart of all of the biting. I write down what happened before my hamster bit us, and possible explanations for his biting. This is what the chart looks like:

BITING BEHAVIOR

Jeannie touches him	He jumps (is he surprised?)	He bites Jeannie (me)
The car accident	He jumps (is he scared?)	He bites Jeannie (me)
Alistair pokes him	He jumps (is he scared?)	He bites Alistair
Mom scratches him under the chin	Is he ticklish?	He bites Mom

I can see a pattern here. Harvey Owens bites when he is surprised or scared. He also bites when people touch him in ways he doesn't like being touched.

I think about what I do when I'm surprised or scared. Or mad.

I take another sheet of paper and I make a sign. I tape the sign onto the wall above Harvey's cage. Here is what it says:

1. I do not like being poked.
2. I do not like being tickled.
3. I do not like being scared.
4. I do not like being surprised.

If these things happen I will bite.

Be nice to me and I will be nice to you.
These are the Rules.

Tomorrow I will show the sign to Mom. I will also show the sign to Alistair. And when Dad comes, I will show the sign to Dad.

Then I hear something from the next room. It sounds like Alistair is crying. I've heard him before, but not quite this loud.

I get out of bed. I take Harvey Owens out of his cage, and I go into Alistair's room. He stops crying as soon as I'm in there but he keeps sort of snuffling.

"Here," I say, putting Harvey Owens on Alistair's quilt. "Smell him."

"What are you talking about?" says Alistair in a squeaky voice.

"Just put your face on him. It helps," I say.

Alistair gently puts his face on Harvey Owens.

"He's soft," says Alistair. "He's like dandelion fluff." My brother's voice isn't so squeaky anymore.

"He has forest fur," I say. "He smells good, right?"

"He smells like wood chips," mumbles Alistair.

When Alistair lifts his head, I pick up Harvey Owens and start back to my room.

"Good night, Ear," says Alistair.

"Good night, Nose," I say.

CHAPTER FOURTEEN

SAPPHIRE

It is dark. It is quiet. I am back in my cage and I listen. I hear Alistair's even breathing from the other room. I hear Jeannie's even breathing from her bed nearby. It might be a good time to look for an *Exit* but I am too tired. I am just too tired for that.

I dig around in the wood shavings and make a nice little nest. It is *Very Fresh*. I curl up.

This would be a good time to be nocturnal.

But I just cannot do it.

CHAPTER FIFTEEN

JEANNIE

When I wake up, it's 9:00 a.m. on Monday, and I'm already late for school.

"WHY DIDN'T SOMEONE WAKE ME?" I yell.

Alistair stumbles out into the hallway.

"What's going on?" he says. "Where's Mom?"

"What the heck!" she says, coming out of her room. She's still in her nightgown.

"I'm going to be sooo late!" I say. "First I have to feed my hamster and then I've got to finish my homework."

"It's a little late for your homework," says Alistair snarkily.

"I'll call the school and tell them you'll both be there in half an hour," Mom says.

"WHAT ABOUT HARVEY OWENS? WHAT ABOUT MY HOMEWORK?"

"Never mind," she answers. "Just get ready. And stop yelling! I can hear you just fine!"

"You can hear but you don't LISTEN," I say. "WHAT ABOUT—"

"Never mind!" yells Mom. "Just do as I say! Grab some toast and get dressed! And be ready for the taxi in fifteen minutes!" Then she says a swear word.

I look at Alistair. He is looking at me. We turn around and go into our bedrooms. I shut my door. First I'm going to feed Harvey Owens. First things first.

Harvey Owens is curled up in a nest of wood shavings.

"Good boy," I say. My heart is beating so hard that I wonder if Harvey Owens can hear it.

I put some pellets into his food dish and then go out to the kitchen for some vegetables. Mom is standing in her slippers by the sink. She is *still* wearing her nightgown.

"I smell burnt toast," calls Alistair.

"Get dressed right now!" Mom yells. "I'm late for work!" And then she says the swear word again.

I grab a carrot and run back to my bedroom. Harvey Owens is still asleep. I gently stroke the top of his head and he opens one eye.

"Good boy," I say. "Breakfast time."

He opens the other eye. I take a deep breath and smile at him. I think he smiles back. Then he scampers over to his food bowl.

"Jeannie!" Mom yells. "What did I tell you to do?"

"Okay, okay," I mutter.

"You have five more minutes and then we are leaving whether you are still in your pajamas or not," she says.

I quickly put on jeans and a sweater. Then I look at Harvey Owens. Will he be all right alone here all day without me? I think about the homework I haven't done.

"I have a stomachache," I call out into the hallway.

"One more minute until the taxi gets here!" Mom hollers.

And that's when I do it. I throw on my jacket and gather up Harvey Owens. Then I tuck him into my coat pocket. Just like that. I tuck him into my pocket and I button the pocket shut.

CHAPTER SIXTEEN

SAPPHIRE

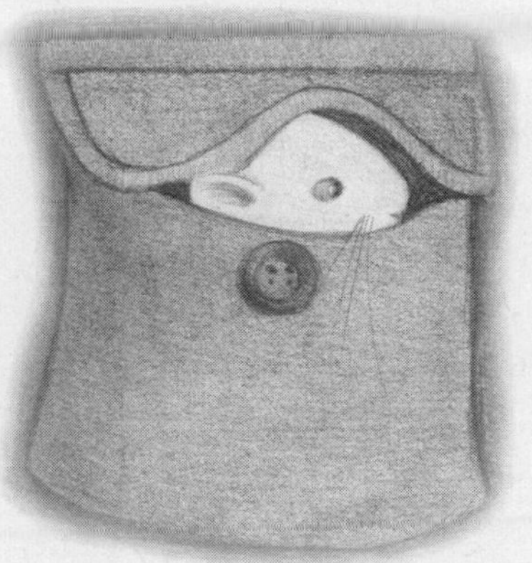

This pocket is warm. And dark. But I can see light coming in through the flap. So it is not so bad. It is not so bad, really. We are swinging along and I kind of like it. I kind of like it in here.

I sing.

I sing a swinging song.

Swing high.
Swing low.
Low high.
High low.

CHAPTER SEVENTEEN

JEANNIE

When I get to school, it's clear that we are really late. There is no one on the playground. There is no one in the hallway, either.

I leave Alistair at the door and go straight to my classroom. It's buzzing with activity.

"Welcome, Jeannie!" says Mr. Kloppenheim. His mustache always wiggles from side to side when he talks. "Go leave your coat in your locker, please."

"But I'm—I'm cold!" I say.

"Hmmm," says Mr. Kloppenheim. "I hope you're not getting sick."

"Well, I did have a stomachache this morning...," I say.

"Let's get you started with this group project," he tells me. "And see how you feel in a little while."

I leave my coat on. And every now and then I gently touch the pocket. I can feel Harvey Owens in there sleeping. I'm sure he's sleeping. And each time I touch him I feel happy.

Mallory Vanelli is already trying to be the boss of everything.

"Jeannie, you color the shapes on our poster while I add the words," she says.

Coloring. Who wants to do coloring!

"I want to do some of the words too," I say. I know all about this stuff. It's part of our Rocks and Minerals unit.

"You weren't here when we started. So...," she says. "Ashton is cutting the 3D parts. Serena is checking spelling. So you have to color."

"**BUT I WANT TO DO SOME OF THE WORDS,**" I say.

"Everything okay here?" asks Mr. Kloppenheim, looking at us.

"Yes," says Mallory Vanelli.

"Yeah," I say. After Mr. Kloppenheim starts working with another group, I take out my math homework. It's easy and I finish it in just a few minutes. Then I do the coloring on our group's poster. But I don't enjoy it. I gently touch my pocket where Harvey Owens is sleeping.

"Watch what you're doing," says Mallory Vanelli. "Color inside the lines."

I feel my face getting hot. Who does she think she is? She's not the boss of me!

"Want to see what I brought for show-and-tell?" I whisper. I open my pocket. Mallory Vanelli looks into it.

"Ooh!" she breathes. "He's cute!"

Suddenly Harvey Owens wakes up. He bursts out of my pocket, slides down the front of my coat, and lands on the seat of my chair.

"What's that?" says Ashton. "A mouse? IT'S A MOUSE!"

And then everything gets crazy.

CHAPTER EIGHTEEN
SAPPHIRE

This place is very loud! I fling myself onto the floor and once again I am *Free*.

Free!

I see a lot of shiny things. I run. The floor here is slippery. So slippery! I slide under a chair. Then I climb into a running shoe.

"It's in my gym shoe!" someone yells.

It?

I see a big, hairy hand coming toward me.

I do the only thing I can think of to do.

I bite.

CHAPTER NINETEEN

JEANNIE

Now I'm sitting by the front door of the school. Harvey Owens is in an empty donut box on my lap. My teacher is in the secretary's office getting a Band-Aid.

"WHY CAN'T HE JUST STAY AT SCHOOL?" I yell. "OTHER PEOPLE HAVE BROUGHT PETS TO SCHOOL."

"They always asked permission," Mr. Kloppenheim says when he comes out of the office. His mustache is wiggling like crazy as he talks. "And their animals don't bite."

"HARVEY OWENS DOESN'T BITE," I yell. "Well, only when someone breaks the Rules!"

"Harvey Owens," repeats Mr. Kloppenheim. "Isn't that your dad's name?"

Then, without even meaning to, I start to cry. I cry so loudly that the secretary comes out of his office with a box of Kleenex. And then suddenly even the principal is there.

Somehow I am telling them all about it. I tell them about my dad leaving and how he doesn't even come back to visit. And I tell them about waiting and waiting and almost never getting to buy my hamster even though it was all my own money. And I tell them about our car accident. And then I start talking about Harvey Owens and the Rules.

And then my mother is in the hallway.

"What in heaven's name is going on?" she asks.

"EVERYBODY'S BREAKING THE RULES," I say.

But nobody listens. Soon I am sitting in the back seat of Anna Conda's big white truck.

"She saw me waiting for a taxi and offered to help," Mom explains.

"Are you checking that the lid is closed nice and tight?" Anna says loudly, looking at the donut box on my lap. "Because we wouldn't want to see that...that hamster—"

"It's closed tight," I say, smoothing it over with my hand and staring at Anna. She does look like a man. Except today she doesn't have any whiskers on her chin.

When we get to our house, Mom invites Anna in.

"No. I think you and Jeannie better sort things out," Anna booms. "But I'll drop off something for supper. I've been at the grocery store, and today is one of my Big Cooking Days. Do you like cabbage rolls? And pierogies?"

"That would be very thoughtful," Mom says. "I just haven't had the energy for much shopping or cooking." She keeps talking to Anna and I grab her house key and run inside. I don't want Harvey Owens to get a chill.

But when I open the box, I see that something terrible has happened.

HARVEY OWENS IS GONE.

CHAPTER TWENTY

SAPPHIRE

It did not take me long to find a little hole in the bottom corner of the box. And a little hole can become a bigger hole very easily. Especially when you are extremely hyper from eating donut crumbs. When there was a big-enough hole, I thought about an *Exit!* And finding my purpose! And doing something great.

First I nosed around Jeannie's boots but she was talking to her teacher and did not see me. Then I scampered down the hallway. I am still in the hallway and now I am running toward a big white light.

"Do not go toward the light," my mother used to say. That is the only thing I remember her telling me, ever. "Do not go toward the light. If you are running and there is a light, go the other way." I remember her saying that very, very clearly. But I just keep running toward the light anyway.

I soon discover that the light is coming from a big window facing out onto a white field. I am not sure if the light is actually coming from the sky or from the field, but it is a bright light and I am drawn to it. *Be Free,* I think. *This is the way to Be Free.* I press my face against the window.

A bell rings and the hallway fills with kids. They are wearing hats and coats and they are heading toward the door. And then I see them outside. I see them running on the field. I watch the door carefully, and the next time it opens, I run through it.

And now I am outside. There is no ceiling. There are no walls. There are no other doors. I have done it! I *Am Free!*

CHAPTER TWENTY-ONE

JEANNIE

Anna Conda has unlocked her truck and I am looking everywhere, but I don't see Harvey Owens.

"Harvey Owens!" I call. "Are you in here?"

"Come on, Ford!" Anna hollers from where she is standing quite far away on the sidewalk. "Help my friend find her little hamster, will you?"

After a while I know it's time to give up. Harvey Owens isn't here. And if he's not here, that means he's probably back at school.

"You are sure he is not inside the truck anywhere?" Anna asks. "He is not peeking out from under a seat or in the cup holder? Did you check the cup holder? Is he in there?"

She waits until I shake my head before she comes anywhere near the truck. I think she is afraid of my hamster but doesn't want to say it.

"I can take you back there," Anna says. "Do you want us to take you back to the school, me and Ford?"

"Yes!" I say. "We've got to go back there right now! Harvey Owens might be in terrible danger!"

"I'll phone the school," Mom says. "Maybe they've found him already."

"Tell them not to hurt him!" I say. "Tell them to keep him safe until I get there!"

But when Mom phones the school, they say they haven't seen any hamsters on the loose. And they promise they will look for him right after lunch.

"Well, we've done all we can do," Mom says.

"No!" I tell her. "We haven't done all we can do! If I were a hamster in a school, I wouldn't go near JUST ANYONE, that's for certain. I'd keep away. I'd keep away until I saw someone I knew. So Harvey Owens will probably keep away from everybody until I get there!"

"I am at your service," says Anna, saluting me. Her gold skating watch gleams in the sunlight. "Me and Ford will take you back there right now."

"We can't keep you tied up all day," says Mom. "This whole hamster thing is getting just a little bit too ridiculous..."

"WE HAVE TO GO BACK FOR HARVEY OWENS," I yell. "WE JUST HAVE TO."

"All right, Jeannie," Mom snaps. "All right! But you don't have to yell."

"ACTUALLY, IT APPEARS THAT I DO," I shout.

"She's got a point," says Anna mildly. And that's when I start liking Anna. I start liking Anna a lot.

CHAPTER TWENTY-TWO

SAPPHIRE

None of the kids on the playground look like Jeannie.

I do not know why I am thinking about Jeannie when I am supposed to *Be Free*. But I am. I am thinking about her so hard that she is filling my head with herself.

The field stretches ahead of me and I start climbing over crusty white hills, looking far into the distance and breathing in air that is not under any ceiling. It is not under any ceiling and it is not between any walls. It is *Free Air*.

I sing to myself.

Free Air.

Free Air.

Being Free.

Being Free.

For a few moments I feel incredibly happy. Pure sunlight hits me like a song. But it is a frozen song.

I start to shiver.

It may be *Free Air* but it is also *Cold Air*. This business of *Being Free* is a bit uncomfortable. I lick at the chilly, white crystals gathering between my claws.

After a few more minutes of traversing hills and valleys I am shivering harder.

This business of *Being Free* is more than just a bit uncomfortable. It is *very* uncomfortable.

I look into the distance again and it is still...distant.

How big is *Free* anyway?

It seems to me that *Free* is just a little bit too big to think about for very long.

Especially when I do not want to stop thinking about Jeannie.

And it is very cold.

I am now shivering so hard that my teeth are scraping against each other. They make a kind of scraping sound as I sing.

Being Free
Being Free
Free Being
Free Being

I realize that this is a song that makes no sense. It is a song that kind of locks me in place. Even though I am *Free*, I am also frozen.

I try to pick up my pace but I find that I am standing still.

I am actually frozen.

I am frozen to the ground.

CHAPTER TWENTY-THREE

JEANNIE

It's all arranged. We help Anna throw the groceries for her Big Cooking Day into our fridge. Then we drop Mom off at work, which is where she wanted to be all along. Then Anna and I roar back to the school. Anna has promised that Ford will drive me home after we find Harvey Owens.

IF *we find Harvey Owens,* my mind is screaming inside my head.

But we have to find him. We just *have* to!

CHAPTER TWENTY-FOUR

SAPPHIRE

Cannot move. Cannot move.

I look desperately around but I recognize no one. None of the kids on the playground look like Jeannie.

But one of them looks like Alistair! The boy that looks like Alistair is standing at the edge of the playground. I stare at him. It *is* Alistair! He is standing at the edge of the playground as if he wishes he were not there. Kids are playing and talking all around him but nobody talks to him.

After a while the bell rings again. Kids start running past me and I have to lean back and forth to avoid getting bumped.

The last one to come near me is Alistair. He is walking with his head down, dragging his feet.

Hey! I yell. *Look out!*

But he does not look out and his big boot squishes my little tail.

EEEOWWWWWCH! I scream.

Alistair jumps back. He looks down. Then he leans over and gently digs me out of the snow.

"Is it really you?" he asks, sliding off his mitten so that I am draped across his fingers.

I blink my eyes and shiver against the warmth of his hand.

I do not want to *Be Free*. I want to go inside.

But if I do that, what will become of me? If the goal is not *Freedom*, what is the goal?

What is my purpose?

I do what I always do when faced with trauma so great that biting is not an option.

My eyes shut. I sleep.

As if from a great distance I hear Alistair shouting.

"He's dead! He's dead and I think I killed him! I killed Harvey Owens!"

But my eyes are heavy and I do not open them.

CHAPTER TWENTY-FIVE

JEANNIE

Anna parks in the loading zone at the front of the school and I jump out.

"I'll wait right here," she says, pulling her scarf tighter around her neck. "Take your time and let me know if I can help."

"Don't you want to come inside?" I ask.

"No, I think it's better if I stay out here. Sometimes...it'll be better for you if I don't come along," she says.

I shut the door of the truck and run toward the school. It's funny how Anna can be so afraid of a little hamster that she doesn't even want to come into the school with me.

When I get inside, the principal is there waiting. "I'm glad you've come back, Jeannie," she says. "But we don't have any news yet."

"He'll be very frightened," I say. "He's probably hiding somewhere and when he sees me he'll come out."

I walk very slowly up and down the front hallway, holding the hamster cage and calling softly.

"Harvey Owens? Harvey Owens?"

It starts to sound like a little song.

"Harvey Owens.
Harvey Owens.
Owens Harvey.
Owens Harvey."

After I go up and down the front hallway three times, I turn the corner into the main hallway. Lunch recess is just over and kids are everywhere. I know for certain that Harvey Owens would be scared in here.

I tiptoe to the far end of the school and go into the boot room. Most of the kids are back in their classrooms, now, and it's quieter.

"Harvey?" I call gently. "Harvey Owens?"

Suddenly the outside door bursts open and Alistair is there. He is holding something in one hand.

"I found him!" Alistair says. "I found him! In the snow! And I think—I think I might have killed him!"

He's crying but it's not the kind of crying I've heard at home. It's the silent kind. Tears are streaming down his face and dripping onto a little mound of white fur that he's cupping in one palm.

"Harvey Owens!" I say, reaching out for my hamster.

Alistair doesn't want to give him up.

"He's dead," sobs Alistair. "I know he's dead."

"What's going on?" says a boy who's been lingering nearby. "What's that in your hand?"

"Watch out!" Alistair says. "Careful. Don't touch!"

"What is it?" asks the boy.

"My hamster," says Alistair. "Actually, my sister's hamster, to be exact. But—we think...I think—"

CHAPTER TWENTY-SIX
SAPPHIRE

I open my eyes. I see three faces looming over me. There's Jeannie. There's Alistair. And there's another kid. All three of them are looking worried. Then Alistair yells, "This hamster's not dead!"

"I had a hamster once," the other kid says. "And I know a lot about them. Can I have a look?" He takes me into his hands and strokes me gently.

"She's beautiful," he breathes. "She's so beautiful!"

I blink my eyes. *Yes! Yes, that's right!*

Jeannie takes me and holds me against her chest and I can hear her heart beating.

"Can I have another turn?" the kid asks.

"A turn?" says Alistair.

"To hold her? She's a girl, right?"

I blink my eyes, **YES**.

"Just a minute," says Jeannie, resting her cheek against my fur. "Just a minute, okay?"

"What's going on here?" asks a woman.

"I found my sister's hamster," Alistair says. "Out *in the middle of the playground!* And I knew that wasn't good, so..."

I start shivering again. In the middle of the playground! So that's where I was! That's where it is to *Be Free!*

"Oh, thank goodness!" says the woman. "Your mom called us just a few minutes ago to check. She'll be so relieved."

"She is so beautiful," the kid repeats. "What's her name?"

"Harvey Owens," says Jeannie.

"But that's a boy's name!" the kid says.

"Well...," says Jeannie.

"And she's a girl, right?"

"Well...," Jeannie repeats.

I keep blinking my eyes but nobody notices.

The woman asks Jeannie if she might hold me for a minute and then she collects me carefully in her large hands.

"She is definitely a girl," says the woman cheerfully. "I should know. As principal of this school, I've seen a lot of hamsters."

"She needs a new name," says the kid. "Something that really suits her."

"Maybe," says Jeannie. "But maybe not."

Alistair and the kid walk ahead of us down the hallway. They are talking to each other about something. A game, I think. And when the kid turns to go into a classroom, Alistair says, "See you on Saturday, Tom?"

"See you, Alistair," the kid says. And just like that, I think Alistair's found a friend.

Jeannie swings my cage back and forth and I see that she has put down new wood shavings. *Very Fresh!* Just for me!

"Alistair and Jeannie," the principal says quietly as she carefully lowers me into the cage. "I heard about what happened with your dad. And I want you to know that we are all here, anytime. Me and your teachers. We're here if either of you need to talk."

She's got her hands around me in the cage. The principal's got her hands around me and now I think she's trying to cover my ears. But I can see. I can still see everything.

Alistair rubs his sleeve across his eyes. He was happy and now he is sad. Jeannie kicks at a chair leg with her boot. She is sad too. I do not want them to feel sad.

I try to get their attention. But they do not look at me. Neither does the principal. But she has still got her hands over my ears.

So I do the only thing I can think of to do.

I bite.

CHAPTER TWENTY-SEVEN

JEANNIE

I bring my supper into my bedroom because Mom says Harvey Owens is IN DISGRACE and *therefore* cannot eat with us at the table. I sit on my bed and look at him.

Her. I look at her.

Harvey Owens is a girl. That's what that kid Tom said. And even the principal said so.

I take a big mouthful of cabbage roll. And chew. And think about Harvey Owens. I mean, I think about my dad. I wish he were here. I wish he were here right now.

I take another bite. Anna is a very good cook. Alistair said she's a man and maybe he's right. But Mom just said people are who they are.

Anna didn't have time to take her groceries home before supper and so she had her Big Cooking Day here, and I helped. First we soaked the cabbage in vinegar. Then we poured boiling water over it. Blanching, it's called. And then we fried ground beef and mixed it with rice and tomato sauce, and rolled it all up in pieces of cabbage. And then we baked it. Presto. Cabbage rolls. And she left us a big pan of them!

I take my plate out to the kitchen, but before I get to the sink, a lot of sauce gets on my fingers and then the plate just flies out of my hands. And it breaks everywhere.

"Jeannie!" Mom yells. "Why can't you be more careful?"

"It's supposed to be unbreakable," I mutter. "We got the unbreakable kind."

"I don't know how I'm supposed to DO everything!" Mom says. "It's easy for HIM to go off and leave ME with all the mess. But WHEN is it going to be my turn? I work all the time and never get ANYWHERE and then TODAY they offered me a promotion...BUT HOW AM I GOING TO ACCEPT A PROMOTION WHEN I CAN'T WORK ON EVENINGS OR WEEKENDS?" She looks at me and then she looks at Alistair. For a minute we don't say anything.

"A promotion?" says Alistair finally. "That means more money, right? How much more money?"

I bend down to pick up the pieces of my plate.

"And maybe then I could have a bigger allowance," I say softly.

"Never mind," says Mom in a voice that sounds as if it's had boiling water poured over it. "I probably can't do it. Sorry, guys. Sorry for blowing my top." She looks at me. "I'll take care of that mess," she says.

"You can do it," I tell her. "I mean you can do the job. You can do the promotion!"

She just shakes her head. And then her phone rings. It's ducks quacking, so I know it's Dad.

"Yes. No. Yes. No. Maybe. Well...okay," she says. When she puts the phone down, she doesn't look at us.

"Dad got back early from his...from his holiday...and he's coming over tonight. He's coming over to see you both. So let's get this mess cleaned up." She grabs some paper towel, bends over, and swipes at the little pieces that I have missed.

I wipe my hands on my shirt and think about the plate. And how broken it is. And how the pieces will never fit back together. And I think about us, the four of us.

The phone rings again but it isn't Dad. This time it's Mallory Vanelli.

"Can I come over and see your hamster?" she asks.

"Not right now," I tell her. "My dad's coming over tonight."

"Your dad doesn't live there?" says Mallory Vanelli.

When I don't answer, she says, "That's just like me. Well, kind of like me. My mom doesn't live with us. But I get to go to her place for summer holidays, and she has a canoe that I can take out into the middle of the lake whenever I want."

"You won't catch many fish in the middle," I say. "And you're not supposed to be in the middle of a lake in a canoe anyway. That's what my dad says."

"It isn't a very big lake," says Mallory Vanelli. Then she asks, "Can I come over tomorrow?"

"I don't know," I tell her. "I'll have to think about it."

"Who was that, honey?" Mom asks after I have put down the phone.

"Mallory Vanelli," I say.

"Oh?" says Mom.

"She wanted to come over tomorrow, but I'm not sure I'm free," I say. "She's always so bossy. Anyway, maybe Dad will come back again tomorrow."

"Don't count on it," says Mom. And all of a sudden her eyes are all red and her face is wet.

I go to my room and take Harvey Owens out of the cage. Then I go back to the kitchen and put her in Mom's lap. Mom takes in little gulps of air for a while, but then she holds Harvey Owens up to her cheek and takes a deep breath.

"It's going to be okay," she says, looking at me and Alistair. "It's going to be okay."

I hear what she says. But something tells me she's wrong.

And I start feeling hungry, but I know I'm not.

CHAPTER TWENTY-EIGHT

SAPPHIRE

When Jeannie's mom puts me back in my cage in Jeannie's room, she pets me a little more. And then I hear Jeannie yelling from the living room.

"Dad! Daddy! Come and see my hamster!" she says.

And then Jeannie, Alistair, and both their parents are in the bedroom looking in at me.

"Wow, look at those eyes!" says their dad. "I've never seen an animal with eyes that blue. I wonder if his mom had blue eyes too."

I blink my eyes as hard as I can.

"It's a girl," says Jeannie. "But I haven't...I haven't actually named her yet."

"You did so!" cries Alistair. "You named it—"

"**SHUT UP,**" yells Jeannie. "**I CAN NAME HER WHATEVER I WANT, AND YOU DON'T GET TO SAY.**"

"Well, ex-cuse me," mutters Alistair.

"How have you guys been?" asks their father. He reaches in and pets me on the head before he closes the lid of the cage.

"Good," say Jeannie and Alistair in unison. But they do not sound as if they mean it. Their mother just looks away.

"Dad, can I have a baby snake?" asks Alistair. "Anna says I could probably find one in the community pasture south of the city, as soon as the snow goes. We could feed it hard-boiled eggs and ground beef. That's what Anna fed hers."

"Dad, what should I call my hamster?" Jeannie asks. "And I lost all his wooden toys somewhere but maybe we can find them!"

"How about Fluffy?" her mom says.

"No!" says Jeannie.

"How about Stink Butt?" says Alistair.

"NO," says Jeannie.

"Or you could call her *Jeannie*," says Alistair.

"I am not calling her after myself!" says Jeannie. "That would be so dumb!"

"Well, we'll have to give it all some thought," says their dad. "Hey, do I smell cabbage rolls?"

"Yes!" Jeannie says. "Anna made them."

"Anna?" asks their father. "Who is this Anna, anyway?"

"She lives just a few blocks away," their mom tells him. "After she retired, she helped at the office during tax season a few times, and that's where I first met her. And since then we've...we kind of got re-acquainted."

"Oh," says their dad. "Well, that's nice."

"Help yourself to the cabbage rolls," their mom continues. "I just need to run the vacuum around the kitchen." She goes over to the closet. "*One of us* had a little accident earlier."

Alistair and Jeannie lead their dad out of the bedroom. When their mom opens Jeannie's closet, she starts yelling.

"Jeannie Owens, come back here right now!" she says.

"Okay, okay!" Jeannie says, bouncing into the bedroom.

Her mother is holding the vacuum in one hand and the lamp in the other. The lamp is still broken.

"How did this happen?" she yells.

Jeannie hangs her head.

"Jeannie Owens, you are going to have to pay for this!" says her mother.

"But if you get a promotion," says Jeannie. "If you get a promotion then...maybe you could pay for it..."

That's when Jeannie's mother gets even louder. And Jeannie gets very loud back. And suddenly they are both very loud together.

Then Jeannie takes me out of my cage again and holds me for a little while. Then she gives me to her mother, and *she* holds me for a little while. And by this time, they are both talking quietly again.

"I am who I am," Jeannie says.

"Well, that's accurate," says Mom. "And I love you truly. But you *are* going to pay for that lamp. And you're also going to start doing more chores around here. In fact, you're going to vacuum the kitchen floor right now." Jeannie puts me back in my cage and closes the lid. And my cage feels even bigger than it did before. I don't know how that happens. Once, not so long ago, my cage felt very, very small. So small that I was always looking for an *Exit*, and a way to *Be Free*.

But for some strange reason my cage doesn't feel small anymore.

CHAPTER TWENTY-NINE

JEANNIE

On Saturday the doorbell rings. I run to open it but Alistair gets there first.

"Hi," he says.

It's Tom, the kid from school. "Hi," he says to us.

"Wanna play that game?" Alistair asks.

"Sure," says the kid, and follows Alistair into his room.

"No sisters allowed," says Alistair as he shuts his door.

"That's not fair!" I say. "I CAN PLAY TOO."

"Jeannie, why don't you help me sort the tax files," says Mom. "I could use someone who's good at math."

"I'm good at math," I say. "But I don't really want to help.

You could get Anna to help. She helped you once already during tax season. I heard you say it to Dad."

"What do you want to do?" asks Mom.

"Dad said he might take me skating today," I tell her.

"Maybe. We'll see," says Mom. "He hasn't said for sure because he has a work thing going on. But Anna might come by this afternoon to watch you so I can go into the office for a bit."

"Can she make supper?" I ask. "She cooks better than we do."

"We'll see," Mom says again. At first she looks kind of mad, but then she smiles. "Those prune pierogies were to die for."

"Maybe I could have a friend over too?" I ask.

"Go ahead," Mom answers.

I pick up the phone and punch in Mallory Vanelli's number.

"It's me," I tell her. "Do you want to come over and see my hamster?"

"Right now?" asks Mallory Vanelli.

"Yeah."

"I'll be right there!" she says. In three minutes she's pounding on our door. Trust Mallory Vanelli to pound instead of ringing the doorbell.

I carry my hamster to the living-room couch and then we take turns holding her.

"She's so soft!" Mallory says.

"It's because of all the fur," I tell her.

"And her eyes are so blue!" Mallory says.

"Her mother's eyes were probably blue, as well," I say.

"What's her name?" Mallory asks.

That's when I go silent.

"Haven't you named her yet?" Mallory asks.

I shrug. It's hard to name a hamster when you already had a name for him.

"What about Fluffball!" says Mallory. "Or Puffball! Or Kloppenheim, after our teacher!"

I wonder what Mr. Kloppenheim would say about that. We break into giggles.

"Maybe something a little more...sparkly," I say.

"How about Twinkle Toes?" asks Mallory. "Or Glitter Princess!"

"I'm thinking more about rocks and minerals," I tell her.

"Quartz?" suggests Mallory. "She's white, like Quartz!"

"Mmm, maybe something like that," I say. "Alabaster?"

"Opal?"

"Moonstone?"

"Diamond?"

Mallory holds my hamster up to her face.

"It's her eyes I like best. Her sparkly blue eyes."

"What about Sapphire?" I say. "Sapphire Owens!"

The hamster blinks her eyes. She blinks them hard.

"Yes!" says Mallory. "Yes, that's it!"

We play with Sapphire for a while, and then we go into my room and get out my paper dolls. They used to be Mom's but now they are mine and they have clothes from the eighties, with real shoulder pads and everything. Mallory and I are really too old for paper dolls, but it turns out that we both like to play with these ones.

"You be the dad and children and I'll be the mom," I tell Mallory.

"No, I want to be the mom," she says. "She's got the best clothes."

"I know," I say. "But they're my dolls. So we should play with them however I say."

"No, that's not fair." Mallory looks at me and her eyebrows are cross. "You're being bossy."

"Hey, do either of you want a small snack?" calls a voice from the kitchen.

"No thanks, Anna," I call back.

"Wait, maybe I do," says Mallory. She goes out to the kitchen and I follow.

"It could be a small snack or a big snack," booms Anna, holding a wooden spoon above a bowl that looks like it has cookie dough in it.

"What are you making?" asks Mallory.

Anna rubs her chin. It's bristly again.

"Well, it could be cookies or it could be bigger than that. Cookie pizzas!" she says.

"That's not your mom," Mallory says to me.

"I am Anna Conda," says Anna. "Master Chef of this household, at least for today."

I giggle. But Mallory doesn't laugh. She just stares at Anna. Then she whispers, "She's a man, right? A man who dresses like a woman?"

I shrug.

"She's just Anna," I tell her.

I watch as the cookies—two huge ones—get put into the oven. Mallory seems awfully quiet.

"I think I'd better go home now," Mallory says finally. "I might—my mom might need me to come home."

"I thought you said you didn't live with your mom," I say, a little more loudly than I mean to.

"I still have to go!" says Mallory Vanelli.

"Is it about the dolls? Because we can play with them a different way—" I begin, following her into the hallway.

"It's not about your stupid dolls!" yells Mallory Vanelli.

"Well, what *is* it about?" I ask.

"I just don't like that man-woman," she answers. "Ask me back when she's not here."

"Well, that'll never happen," I say. "Anna's probably going to be here a lot. Anyway, I like her."

I'm thinking of all the things I like about Anna, but

before I start listing them off, Mallory yanks open the front door.

"I just have to go!" she says.

And she does.

CHAPTER THIRTY

SAPPHIRE

I am waiting in my cage and it is like I am waiting for something but I do not know what.

I used to be waiting for an *Exit* to *Be Free*. But I am not waiting for those things anymore. I do not need an *Exit* to be happy.

But I am still waiting for something. Because even though I can be happy here, I am not happy. And it is the "me" part that I need to figure out, not the "here" part.

There are voices outside Jeannie's bedroom and they are not happy voices. They are rising, angry voices and then a door slams and then there are quiet voices. But the quiet voices are sad.

And I wait here and wonder:
What is my purpose?

CHAPTER THIRTY-ONE

JEANNIE

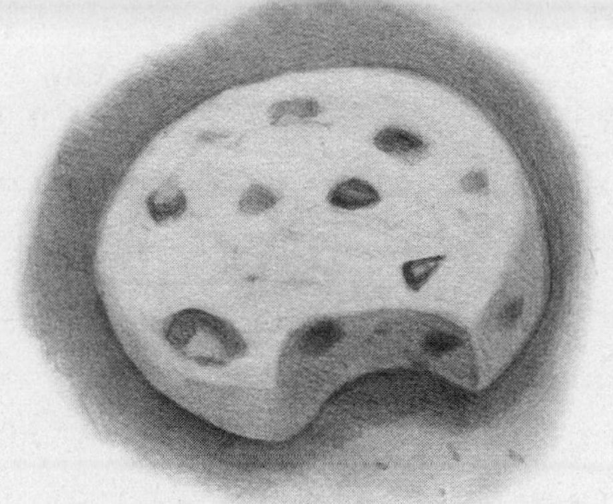

"I don't understand what you mean," I say to Anna for the second time.

"I am sorry I made your friend leave," she repeats.

"You didn't make her. She left because of her own self," I say.

"If I hadn't been here, she would have stayed, yes?" Anna says. "And you could have had a happy afternoon together."

I look at Anna. Her face is kind. Her eyes are sad. I stare at the bristles on her chin, but I don't mind about them. They are part of her.

"It happens," Anna goes on. "Sometimes people just decide they don't want to know me."

"Why did you change your name?" I ask.

"What?" she says.

"When we were in your truck, you said that you paid for a name change. And that your parents had called you something else."

"Did I say that?" Anna says. She kind of smiles, but it's a sorrowful smile. "Oh well, maybe I did. But anyway. Would you like a cookie? I think they're ready." She goes to the oven and heaves open the door.

"What was your old name?" I ask. "I won't tell anyone."

"Well, it isn't a secret, really," Anna says, pulling out the tray of cookies and then coming back to sit down at the table.

"It isn't really a secret, but there are people that wouldn't understand," she continues. "I've kind of given up on them."

"I'll understand," I say.

Anna looks at me for a minute, as if she is measuring me.

"Don't give up," I tell her. "You can't give up."

Then she says, "My first name was William. And my last name was Anderson. William Ford Anderson. Just like that. You see, not a bad name. But in the end a terrible name for me." She sighs.

"Like Harvey Owens wasn't a good name for Sapphire," I say.

"Yes. Kind of like that," Anna says.

"But you kept Ford," I tell her.

"What?"

"You kept the name Ford. For your truck," I say.

"Ah, yes. Yes, you are correct. It is true. I did just that. I always buy Ford trucks for that very reason."

I stare at Anna for a minute.

And then I say, "When you didn't come into the school with me, it wasn't because you were afraid of my hamster, was it?"

Anna looks down at her hands.

"Well," she says, "I actually am…I truly am afraid of hamsters. And mice." She gives a little shiver.

"But when you didn't come into the school with me, when my hamster was lost. You had another reason, didn't you?"

She doesn't answer.

So I know it's true. She didn't want to make things hard for me. She even said that, but I wasn't listening very well. So it's not only Mom who doesn't listen. I feel unhappiness flow from my head down into my stomach.

I get a spatula from the drawer and an oven mitt, and I start taking the cookies off the pan, even though I know it's too soon. They fall apart and I keep on until they end up in crumbs.

"What do you think about it all?" Anna says, finally.

I flip the last piece of cookie from the tray and turn to look at her.

"YOU ARE WHO YOU ARE," I say. And then I say it again, quieter. "You are who you are. And people should understand that."

She smiles but it's still a sad smile.

"Do you want some of those cookies?" she asks.

"Okay," I tell her. And I try to smile but I just can't.

I wish there were Rules for people.

CHAPTER THIRTY-TWO

SAPPHIRE

Jeannie comes in and takes me out of my cage and I can smell the sadness hanging on her like smoke. She lifts me to her cheek and then she sits down on the bed and gently presses me against her heart.

After a few minutes she heaves a big sigh. Then she starts to put me back into my cage but at the last moment she changes direction and takes me out to the kitchen where Anna is doing the dishes.

"Here," says Jeannie, holding me out to Anna.

"No thank you, dear. I just—it looks a little too much like a—"

"Here!" says Jeannie, more insistently. "Take her! You can't decide what to think unless you actually know her first! One step at a time!"

Anna rubs the back of her neck and then she gingerly reaches out with one hand.

"Both hands," says Jeannie.

Anna sits down at the kitchen table and Jeanie puts me into Anna's cupped hands. I sit as still as possible. Anna's hands are shaking. Anna's heart is beating loudly, as if it's stomping around in her chest.

"I bought hamster toys, but I can't find them anywhere," Jeannie says.

"Toys?" asks Anna.

"Wooden ones," says Jeannie. "Because the plastic ones that are cheaper aren't very safe for animals. I read it on the internet."

After a few minutes, Anna relaxes. She pulls me a little closer and looks at me carefully.

"She's really quite...quite beautiful," Anna whispers. "And look at those eyes! They remind me of something. Stars, yes? Blue stars."

"And sapphires," says Jeannie.

"Yes," breathes Anna. "Yes, exactly that!"

CHAPTER THIRTY-THREE

JEANNIE

After Anna has held Sapphire so long that I think they've both gone to sleep, the doorbell rings.

"It's Dad!" I say, looking out the window. "HE'S HERE FOR SKATING!"

But hurrying up the sidewalk behind Dad is another man. Dad turns and the two of them talk for a minute. Anna lets me take Sapphire back to my room and she opens the door.

"Hello," I hear her say. "Hello, Mr. Owens. I'm Anna."

"Thank you for those great cabbage rolls," Dad says.

Then I hear Mom's voice. She's home early! She sounds all excited and kind of mad. How could she be mad? She's only just gotten home and I haven't done anything yet.

"I thought we weren't going to do this until later," she says. "We're not exactly ready."

I shut the lid on Sapphire's cage and then I stand beside my dresser. Something's happening out there but I'm not sure what. I feel like I'm frozen in place. Finally I head down the hallway just as Anna is leaving.

"There's Chicken à la Conda in the oven," she whispers to me. "I've set the timer. Make sure it comes out at six o'clock sharp or it will be roasted to death."

"It's already roasted to death," I say, and Anna grins.

"Just make sure!" she says. So I nod.

She presses something into my hands. It's the hamster toys!

"You found them!" I say.

"Under the table," she smiles. "Never give up!"

After I shut the door behind her, I stand in the porch and wave. Then the voices in the living room get louder.

"My ex needed me to pick up Tomas," I hear the man saying. "And I didn't know the address until she texted me just now. So I didn't realize it was here! I'm so sorry! Maybe we can…" I walk into the room and the man looks at me.

"Hello!" he says, and grins. It's a nice grin. "You must be Jeannie!"

Dad strides over and picks me up, even though I'm really too big to be picked up, and then he sits with me on the couch. He smiles at me and his eyes are crinkling up the way I love. I lean my face against his rough chin.

"We might as well tell them now," Dad says gently, looking at Mom. "I think we are ready." Then he calls, "Alistair? Tomas? Come on out here."

It sounds like it might be about something special. But I know it's not a present or anything like that.

They come out of Alistair's room and Tom says, "Hey, Dad," to the other man. "I thought Mom was going to get me. It's not your weekend."

"She had to go to the hospital," the man says. Then he looks at me and grins again. "She's not sick. She's a doctor. She's on call today and someone decided to have a baby."

I look from Dad, to the man, to Mom, and then back to Alistair and Tom. Then I look again at Dad. Something is going on here but I don't know what. I start fiddling with the hamster toys and press them out of their plastic packages. There's a little wooden bench and a kind of seesaw. I flip the seesaw back and forth and it's just how my stomach is feeling: up and down, up and down.

CHAPTER THIRTY-FOUR

SAPPHIRE

Something is definitely going on around here. They are all in the living room. Jeannie's dad talks for a while and then he stops. And then everyone is quiet. What are they doing out there?

CHAPTER THIRTY-FIVE

JEANNIE

I finally run into my bedroom and put the toys into the hamster cage. Then I bring Sapphire out of the cage and into the living room. I sit down, holding her under my chin.

"So, do you...like...want to be a woman?" I finally ask Dad. "Like Anna wants to be a woman?"

"No, not at all," he says.

"But you...you don't love Mom and you love Tom's dad instead," says Alistair, taking Sapphire and holding her against his chest.

"I love Mom in a different way than I love Tom's dad," says Dad. "Robin. His name is Robin."

"I don't like Robin's aftershave," mumbles Alistair. "It smells like metal going up my nose." I can see him holding Sapphire even tighter.

Dad reaches over and carefully lifts Sapphire out of Alistair's hands. Everybody is quiet for a minute.

"Dad will always be your dad," says Mom. "But he's going to try to be Tom's dad too."

"Two dads!" I say. "That means we can have two dads as well!"

"That's right," says Robin, winking at me.

"Just as long as you don't get to like Robin better than me!" Dad says, smiling.

"I WOULD NEVER," I tell him.

"I don't want two dads," says Alistair flatly. "It's only normal to have one."

"Maybe we could each have two allowances," I begin, but Mom shakes her head.

"The word *normal* doesn't really apply to people," says Tom. "It only applies to the weather and stuff like that."

"It'll take time to get used to things," says Dad. "We'll just take it day by day, okay, Alistair?"

"One day at a time," says Mom, softly.

"Maybe," Alistair says. "But when did it happen? When did everything change? And how come Tom knew about it and we didn't?"

"I met your dad a long time ago," Tom tells him. "I just didn't know he was your dad."

"Will you take me fishing? And skating?" I ask Robin. "That's what I like to do!"

"I'll always be a better skater than Robin!" My dad laughs. Robin laughs as well, and puts his arm around Tom.

"We know it's complicated. But we're going to do our best to make it work," Robin says.

"I'm sorry if it's been hard on all of you," Dad says. Then he adds, more softly, "I know it's been hard on us. But we just have to be...we just have to be who we are."

CHAPTER THIRTY-SIX

SAPPHIRE

I blink. I think about that. I think about that hard.

We just have to be who we are.

Jeannie's dad holds me out to Jeannie's mom and she takes me into Jeannie's bedroom.

"That's about *all* the difficult conversations I can stand for one day," she says softly to me. "How about you?"

She lowers me into my nest of wood shavings. *Very Fresh*. It's always *Very Fresh* in here and I am glad. Not like under that fridge. Not like in the pet store. Nice. Like a home.

Robin comes into the room too.

"I know this isn't how we all planned it would be," he says gently. "But I think it's going to work out."

"It has to," she answers. "It just has to."

Robin comes closer to my cage. I see Robin's hand coming through the lid and hovering close to my head. His hand smells like soap. It is a strong smell. I do the only thing I can think of to do...

CHAPTER THIRTY-SEVEN
JEANNIE

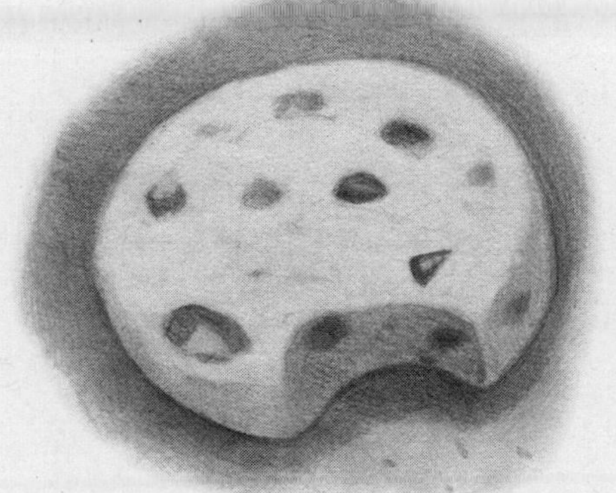

"Stop," I tell Alistair. "It's time to stop asking questions!" Sometimes he doesn't know when to quit.

"But it isn't a separation, is it?" he keeps saying to Dad, now that Robin and Mom have left the room. "It's a divorce, right? It's going to be a divorce?"

"Yes," Dad says, finally. "It is going to be a divorce. But we are working together really well so that I will be spending lots of time with you both, and your mother will be spending lots of time with you both."

"That hasn't happened so far," Alistair says.

"We are trying," Dad replies. "I know it's hard to get used to things changing."

"You used to love Mom when you first married her and then you started loving her in another kind of way," Alistair says. "And now you love Robin and you're probably going to marry *him*. But what's to stop you from loving *him* in another kind of way too?"

"Well, nothing, I guess," says Dad. "Except that Robin and I believe this is a permanent step for us. And we will do our best to make sure that—that you kids have all our support."

"Can I get a drink of water?" asks Tom. "Or juice or something?"

"Absolutely," Dad says, and takes Tom into the kitchen.

"And can I have some of these things?" I hear Tom asking. "Whatever they are?"

"I think they're cookies," Dad answers. "Cookie crumbs, I guess. But absolutely, help yourself."

"It was supposed to be cookie pizza," I call out.

"I'm going back to play my game," mutters Alistair, and then he leaves me on the couch. And I'm sitting here in the living room alone. And I'm wondering. And what I'm wondering about is:

When did Dad switch his love for Mom from the married kind of way to the other kind of way?

Was it sometime when they were fighting?

Was it sometime when they were mad?

Was it sometime when they were mad at me?

I wish there were RULES about this. RULES for people to follow that would MAKE EVERYTHING BETTER.

But I know there aren't.

I look around the room and then I say a little swear word to myself. It doesn't help, so I say it louder. But that doesn't help, either.

CHAPTER THIRTY-EIGHT

SAPPHIRE

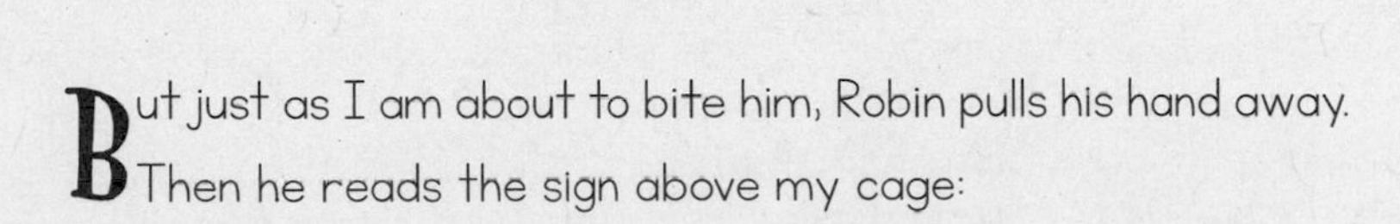

But just as I am about to bite him, Robin pulls his hand away. Then he reads the sign above my cage:

1. I do not like being poked.
2. I do not like being tickled.
3. I do not like being scared.
4. I do not like being surprised.

If these things happen I will bite.

Be nice to me and I will be nice to you.
These are the Rules.

"Makes sense," says Robin. "I'd better pay attention to this."

"I hope you do," snorts Jeannie's mom. "Because if you don't, that hamster **WILL** bite ."

"Sapphire," says Jeannie, running into the room behind them. "**SAPPHIRE!** Sapphire the Great!"

"Sapphire Sharp-Tooth Owens," calls Alistair from his room.

"**SAPPHIRE THE GREAT OWENS**," says Jeannie.

"Lower your voice, Jeannie," says Jeannie's mom. "Or you're going to deafen that animal."

When she says "that animal," I think she means me.

Because I *am* an animal. But even more than that, I am a hamster. And even more than that, I am Sapphire. I am Sapphire the Great.

"*Sapphire the Great,*" Jeannie sings over my cage.

"*Sapphire Owens the Great. Great the Owens Sapphire,*" she sings.

Sapphire the Owens Great, I sing along.

Great Owens the Sapphire.

It is nice to be singing together. We kind of harmonize.

But what is my greatness? What is my greatness, really?

Their mom and Robin go back to the living room and Jeannie stays and pets me.

Then Jeannie runs back to the living room while their mom comes in here again. And she pets me. And then Jeannie's mom goes out and her dad comes in and leans over my cage.

"I'll see you tomorrow, Sapphire," he says.

Tomorrow?

"I'll be back to make supper while Jeannie's mom stays at work," he goes on. "And I hope you like celery, because I'm going to bring you some!"

Tomorrow! When I think about *Tomorrow* my cage feels so big that I think I am actually *Free*. I am actually *Free* in here!

And *Being Free* is what I have always wanted!

But there is something else. There is more to life than *Where*.

It is also about purpose. And greatness.

And I am still not sure about that.

I am still not certain.

What is my purpose in life? What am I good at?

CHAPTER THIRTY-NINE

JEANNIE

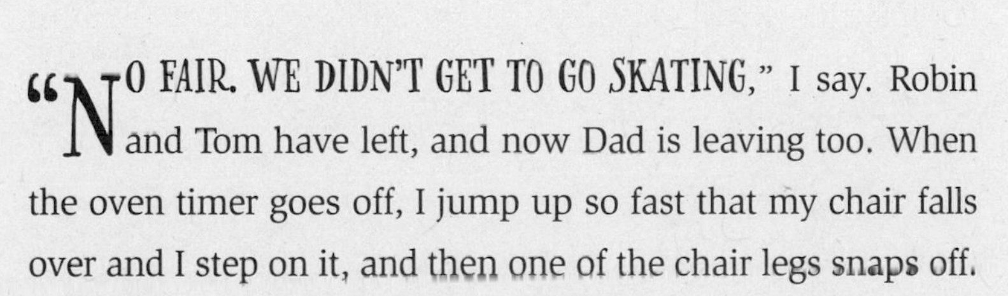

"NO FAIR. WE DIDN'T GET TO GO SKATING," I say. Robin and Tom have left, and now Dad is leaving too. When the oven timer goes off, I jump up so fast that my chair falls over and I step on it, and then one of the chair legs snaps off.

"The Chicken à la Conda is DONE," I yell. "We have to take it out of the oven!"

"Jeannie!" says Mom, looking at the broken chair.

"It was an accident!" I say. "AN ACCIDENT."

"I meant to fix that chair leg before now," says Dad. "Sorry."

"SEE! SEE! IT WASN'T MY FAULT!" I yell.

"I can hear you, Jeannie. You don't have to yell," says Mom.

She uses oven mitts to lift Anna's chicken onto the counter.

"You hear but you don't listen!" I tell her.

"Just try to be a little more graceful," she says. "Before every last thing in this house gets broken."

"I AM WHO I AM," I say. "EVEN IF EVERYTHING IS MY FAULT."

"But everything isn't your fault, Jeannie," Dad says. "You know that, right? You know that everything—all the stuff that's going on with our family—isn't your fault, right?"

"Maybe if I followed the Rules," I mutter. "Maybe if I even knew what the Rules were..."

"No," says Dad, and then Mom comes and puts her arm around me. I feel hot tears fill my eyes.

"No, Jeannie," says Mom. "This isn't your fault, honey. It's just the way it is. I know it's tough for you, but you're a strong, smart girl. We think you can handle it."

"Okay," I say in a small voice. "Okay." My voice sounds like it's coming from far away.

"That doesn't mean you have to feel happy about it," Mom goes on. "But one day at a time, things will start to feel a little more normal."

"Tom says *normal* is just a word for the weather," I tell her.

"Well, maybe he's right," Mom laughs.

"Let's plan on going skating tomorrow afternoon," Dad says after a minute. "I could pick you up from school at two o'clock. It's early dismissal tomorrow, right?"

"Yeah...okay," I answer. "Can Mallory Vanelli come too?"

"I thought you said Mallory Vanelli was too bossy," Mom says.

"Well, sometimes she *is*. But sometimes she *isn't*," I say. "Sometimes...sometimes I guess I'm the bossy one. So... can she come? PLEASE?"

"Okay. Should I call her parents right now?" Dad asks.

"Her dad. You'll have to talk to her dad," I tell him, getting the phone. "And can Sapphire come too?" I add.

"Sapphire? Skating? I think she's happier at home," Dad says. "Anyway, Alistair might need her while we're gone."

"Alistair could come skating," I say, but then I remember how much Alistair hates skating. Alistair hates going anywhere at all. He just wants to play that stupid video game because he's ADDICTED.

Then I have an idea.

"Can Anna come?" I ask. "Anna and Mallory Vanelli?"

Dad looks at me and crinkles up his eyes.

"You're planning something," he says, grinning at me a little suspiciously.

I just shrug and run off to my room because I don't really want to talk about it right now.

But I am planning something. I am planning something really important.

CHAPTER FORTY

SAPPHIRE

When Jeannie's dad comes to the house the next day, I am racing around my cage even though hamsters are supposed to sleep in the daytime.

I am racing around my cage and Jeannie's dad comes into her room and gets her skates from the closet. Then he drops some celery into my food bowl.

"You like celery, don't you?" he says as I charge over and begin eating.

"Thanks for taking care of everyone, Sapphire," he says. "I really mean it."

I look up at him, not sure I am hearing him correctly over

all the crunching. I stop chewing, a string of celery hanging from my jaws.

"Thanks," he says again.

Thanks?

Taking care of everyone?

Is that what I have been doing?

CHAPTER FORTY-ONE

JEANNIE

Dad ties my skates really tight, just the way I like them. He ties Mallory Vanelli's skates too, and we stomp down the rubber hallway onto the ice. Mallory's skates are so shiny I think they must be brand new.

I look around but I don't see Anna. She said she might meet us here, but I don't see her. I don't think she's coming, but I keep looking as I coast away from the boards, ahead of Mallory, who is awfully slow.

Suddenly some kids along the side of the rink point and laugh.

"Look at that one! Look at her skate!"

I look around. What are they laughing about? And then I realize they're pointing at us.

Actually, they're pointing at Mallory Vanelli. She's not really skating—she's sort of jogging on the ice. She's lifting her knees and pounding her skates up and down and not really getting anywhere.

Mallory Vanelli doesn't know how to skate. I look at her face. It's all puckered and red. She looks as if she's going to start bawling.

"She looks like a dork!" one of the kids snickers.

And then suddenly there's a big flash of purple between us and those kids. It's like a shooting star, and it blazes across the ice, circles, and returns.

"Whoa!" I hear people say. "Would you look at that!"

It's Anna. She's wearing a sparkly purple skating costume that billows and lifts as she dances across the rink. I've never seen anyone skate so fast, not even my dad. And when she comes back for another round, she jumps into the air right beside us and spins like the inside of a blender.

A few people clap. The kids by the boards lean forward with looks of surprise and awe on their faces.

Mallory Vanelli wobbles and almost falls down, but Anna holds out her hands and Mallory grabs on.

Then Anna takes one of Mallory's elbows and I take the other and we coast her along to the other side of the rink.

"Here is where I give my skating lessons," Anna bellows. "For anyone who wishes to improve, yes? For free," she adds.

Mallory Vanelli stares at her.

"How can you skate like that?" she breathes.

"It's easy," says Anna. "When you have had a little practice." Her smile is kind, shining above the bristles on her chin. The gold watch gleams on her wrist.

"I didn't know it would be so hard," says Mallory wistfully. "I wish I could skate even a little bit. My mom was going to teach me last year, but—" She stops. "I guess she didn't have time."

Mallory is staring down at her skates. She still looks like she is going to cry.

"One step at a time," I say. I look at Anna. Then I look at Mallory.

"Should we have a small skating lesson right now?" asks Anna.

"That's the way," I say.

Mallory looks at me. Then she looks back at Anna. And then she grins.

"Okay," she says. "Okay! I'd like a lesson, Miss...Mrs..."

"Just Anna," Anna Conda tells her in a kind voice. "So let's start with your weight first on one foot, and then the other..."

"Never give up!" I say. And I look at Anna, who blinks and then gives a little nod. I think she understands what I'm really talking about. I know she does. And I'm glad.

Then Dad is bearing down on us from across the ice and just before he gets here, he stops in a spray of snow.

"Who wants to race?" he challenges.

"No fair," I say. "You always win!"

"Maybe I will and maybe I won't," he teases.

I look over at Anna, who is already busy showing Mallory Vanelli how to glide.

"Okay!" I say. "But you have to skate backward."

"Backward!" he groans.

"Yup," I say. "That's the only way I'll have a chance!"

We head across the ice, and the next time I look, Mallory is gliding. Not very well, but she's doing it. And she looks proud of herself.

And I feel proud of myself too.

And the *next* time I look, Mallory Vanelli and Anna are still practicing, but skating along beside them is Tom. And behind the three of them are Robin and Mom. And behind them is Alistair.

Alistair! Alistair is skating!

If you can call it skating. I watch him for a minute. It isn't really skating yet, but it might be. It might be skating if he works at it. He doesn't look happy to be here. But he doesn't look sad, either. He just looks like… himself.

"HELLO, NOSE!" I yell at him across the rink.

Alistair looks up.

"**HELLO, EAR!**" he yells back.

And then he smiles.

I wish Sapphire were here. If Sapphire were here, it would be perfect.

But soon we'll be home. Soon we'll all be home together.

And just at that moment, Dad streaks by me.

"I win!" he yells.

"No fair!" I say. "I wasn't looking!"

"Race again?" he challenges.

"Yes!" I say.

CHAPTER FORTY-TWO

SAPPHIRE

Today began like any other. I traversed the floor of the cage, rating the aspen shavings. I thought, just like I always do: *Very Fresh! Very Fresh! Very Fresh! Very Fresh!* Then I buried my food bowl.

In the food bowl there are two Cheerios, three Rice Krispies, a fragment of apple, a few pieces of celery, and three peanuts. I have been getting quite a few peanuts lately. I believe they are trying to send me a message.

"I love you," Jeannie sang this morning. "I love you. And you love me."

I love you, I warbled along. *And I love celery. And I love peanuts.*

Now the house is quiet. But soon someone will be here. Maybe it will be Jeannie. Or Alistair. Or their mom. Or their dad. Or Robin. Or Tom. Or Anna. Or Mallory Vanelli. And I am waiting. I am waiting for them. I am dizzy now with all that I know. But I am confident that there is more to learn.

I chew on the wooden seesaw. Then I chew on the little wooden bench. Then I sit on the bench. And I look around. And I think about my purpose and my greatness and my Freedom. In all the excitement I have forgotten where I buried my food bowl. Soon I will look for it. And when I find it, I will eat the Cheerios, the Rice Krispies, the celery, and the fragment of apple. But I will save the peanuts.

Because that is my choice.

And while I am waiting for someone, I might eat one of those peanuts.

Or not.

SAPPHIRE'S
HAMSTER CARE GUIDE

by SAPPHIRE the GREAT (Author)

THIS is HOW **HAMSTERS** Like to BE PETTED

1. Tame hamsters like me enjoy frequent petting. This means petting us **BE-FORE** breakfast...**AFTER** breakfast... mid-morning...**BEFORE** lunch...**AFTER** lunch...mid-afternoon...**BEFORE** supper...**AFTER** supper...and throughout the evening...

2. ...unless we are asleep. Do not pet us when we are asleep. If we are asleep it means we want to **SLEEP!**

3 Be **GENTLE** at all times. Handle us with love!

4 Alternate petting with scratching.

5. Try and find the spots where we like to be scratched, such as behind the ears and along the shoulder blades...

6. **ESPECIALLY** along the shoulder blades!

THIS is WHAT **HAMSTERS** Need to EAT and DRINK

1. Hamsters like me should only eat Healthy Food. This means **OFFICIAL** food from the pet store in a package that says **"HAMSTER FOOD."**

2. We also like (some, not all) **FRESH** fruits and vegetables...

3. ...and Cheerios and Rice Krispies and unsalted peanuts (**MMMMM**, peanuts!).

4. Here are my favorite **FRESH** Foods:

   apples (**ESPECIALLY** McIntosh!)
   bok choy
   broccoli
   carrots
   cauliflower (but **TOO** much gives me flatulence)
   celery
   cucumbers
   dandelion leaves (as long as they have **NOT** been sprayed)
   kale

5. And don't forget **FRESH, VERY FRESH WATER!** Keep our water bottles clean and full.

THIS is WHAT **HAMSTERS** WANT in THEIR HOMES

1. **EVERYONE** needs a little fun! Hamsters love to use exercise wheels just like people use treadmills.

2. Hamsters also like rolling around in hamster-balls (but **NOT** down the stairs–that **HURTS!**). People like rolling around too, but not in people-balls. Maybe people-balls have not been invented yet!

3. Hamsters need other **TOYS** to play with and to chew on. We love to chew! Toilet rolls are all right for some hamsters, but they disappear quite rapidly, so you might run out. **OFFICIAL WOODEN** toys from the pet store are my favorite.

4. Hamsters like me love **FRESH, VERY FRESH** wood chips. Pine is fine for me, but some extra-delicate hamsters need aspen chips. You should get wood chips from the pet store.

5. Hamsters need a special place to sleep. We love soft, re-cycled paper that we can shred into great nest material. Guess where you can get that...at the **PET STORE!**

Thank you for reading my **HAMSTER CARE GUIDE**

Kind regards,

SAPPHIRE the GREAT (Author)

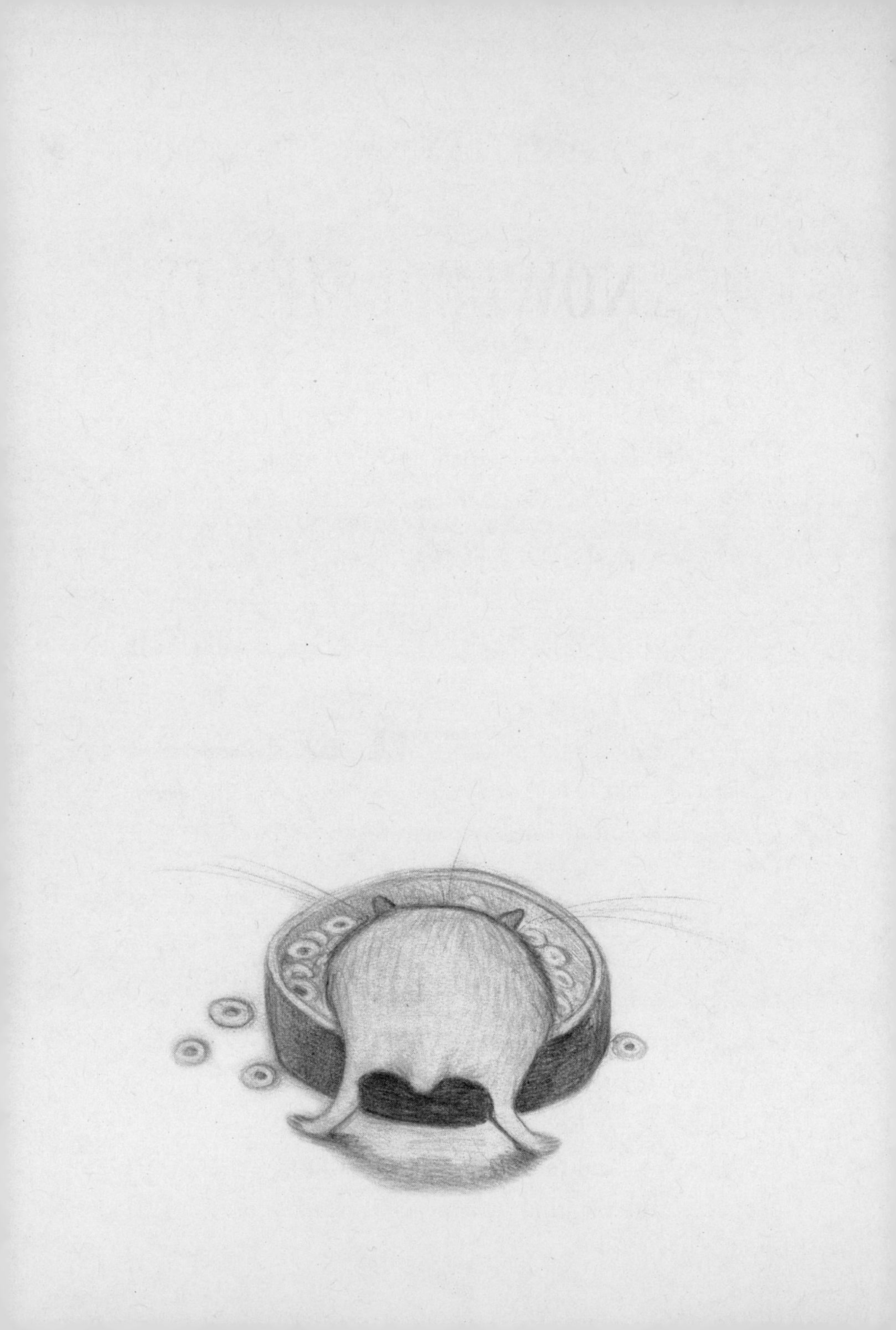

ACKNOWLEDGMENTS

Special thanks to my wonderful editor, Ann Featherstone, and the team at Pajama Press for their fine collaborative work. Thanks also to Patti Rowley for the gift of the magic reading glasses as well as her encouraging words about Anna Conda. Indebtedness to Heike Heimann for the bookends, many years ago, that continually demand new writing, as well as the tutorial on personalized ringtones. Appreciation to the University of Saskatchewan and, in particular, the College of Education for supporting my artistic work. And recognition to OUTSaskatoon for your dedicated and inspiring service to our community.

Gratitude also to a gerbil named Harold Pinter from one of my other books, who also spent time under the refigerator and has been clamoring so long for a sidekick. For him and because of him, I created Sapphire. As well, I must credit the writing of Paulo Freire in *Pedagogy of the Oppressed*, as it has led me to dwell upon the theme of liberation.

And hugs to the family of the real Sapphire for generously sharing hamster wisdom!

AND, as always, thanks to my family for their everlasting love and support, especially my husband and best first-draft and any-draft listener, Dwayne.

WITHDRAWN
No longer the property of the
Boston Public Library.
Sale of this material benefits the Library.